The Giggle-a-Day Joke Book

First published in Great Britain by Collins in 2001
Collins is an imprint of HarperCollins*Publishers* Ltd
77-85 Fulham Palace Road, Hammersmith, London W6 8JB

The HarperCollins*Children'sBooks* website address is
www.harpercollinschildrensbooks.co.uk

5 7 9 8 6 4

Compilation copyright © HarperCollins*Publishers* Ltd 2001
Text copyright © **Child Of Achievement**™ **Awards** 2001
Illustrations by Sue Heap
Cover illustration by Nick Sharratt

ISBN 0 00 711591 1

Printed in Great Britain by
Clays Ltd, St Ives plc

All royalties from the sale of this book go to:
The Child Of Achievement™ **Awards**
Annually presenting 150 Awards and **giving** 150 grants to help **children**
achieve **more** in all walks of life.
Registered Charity No 327-871

The Giggle-a-Day Joke Book

Child Of Achievement™ Awards

Airtours Charity of the Year
The Holiday Makers

Illustrated by Sue Heap

Collins

An imprint of HarperCollins*Publishers*

★ ★ ★
★ INTRODUCTION ★

The postman climbed the steep outside steps to our office with a large sack of mail. As I opened the door he said, 'Nomination forms?' They are pretty good, our Post Office. They deliver nearly 10,000 nomination forms a year – some simply addressed 'Child Of Achievement Awards', some without stamps.

'No,' I said, 'I don't think so.'

The next day, with a similar size bag but a more enquiring voice, he asked, 'Requests for grants, is it?' with a knowing look. The Charity receives thousands of requests for grants. We give 150 every year, ranging from hundreds to thousands of pounds, to help children achieve more.

'No,' I said, 'I don't think so.'

The next time we met, the postbag was just as big – and so was the postman's determination. If he was going to lug bulging sacks up the stairway, his curiosity had to be satisfied. Putting the bag on the step, he asked, 'Is it an appeal?'

'No,' I replied, 'It's a joke book.'

'You're having a laugh, aren't you?' came the response.

'We certainly hope to,' I said. 'The more people laugh, the more joke books will be bought, and the more money the Charity will receive.' Determined to prove my point, I asked him to pick an envelope from the sack. He delved in like a child at a lucky dip and produced a brown envelope. It turned out to be an electricity bill! Despite being given so many things for nothing, we too still have to pay for the basics in life. But the postman seemed strangely satisfied. However, I was reluctant to let the challenge drop. I plunged my hand in and brought out an envelope that looked as if it was going to be a great laugh inside. I was proved right – out came not just one joke, but pages and pages from one of our Award winners.

'Who sent that, then?' he asked.

'One of our Award winners,' I said.

'But they've won Awards because they all have really serious things wrong with them. Or they've helped their mums and families if they are ill. I know, because I read about some in the papers, and in that Yearbook you have. And of course...' he said with a smile of a man who knows a thing or two, 'I've visited your website too, www.childofachievement.co.uk. How can those children feel like writing jokes?'

'But that's just the point.' I said. 'If the children, with all their problems, can still have a laugh at life, don't we owe it to them and their school friends, who've also sent in jokes, to make this the best joke book ever? It's not just in aid of the Charity – it's written by the children themselves.'

'Here,' he said, 'let me see that joke.'

I handed the page over.

My teacher does bird impressions.
What does she do – whistle like a canary?
No, she watches me like a hawk!

The joke was from eight-year-old Laurence McGivern, who had had his legs amputated below the knee when he was little, yet had gone on to compete and win commendations in Irish Dance competitions.

'Sums it all up,' the postman said. 'That bag won't be quite so heavy next time I bring it up. I'll carry it with a lighter heart, on condition you give me a laugh a day.'

'Call it a giggle-a-day,' I said, 'and you've got yourself a deal.'

JULIE FISHER
Founder
Child Of Achievement™ Awards

Monday's jokes are about ghosts,
ghouls, monsters... and school!
That's because Mondays are moandays!

GHOSTS, GHOULS AND MONSTERS

What's a ghost's favourite day of the week?
Moanday!
Laura Hoare

What do werewolves write at the end of their
letters?
Best vicious!
Alex Cottee

Why did the teacher send Dracula's son home?
Because he was coffin too much!
Nafisa Hussain

Which monster can sit on the end of your finger?
The bogeyman!
Carl Smith

What kind of music does a Mummy listen to?
Wrap!
Tara Littlehales

What happens when you have identical twin witches?
You can't tell which witch is which!
Helen Innes

Who did Dracula marry?
The girl necks door!
Kirsty Moore

What kind of mail does a superstar vampire get?
Fang-mail!
Lindzy Westmoreland

What climbs ropes and is wrapped in a plastic bag?
The lunchpack of Notre Dame!
Jack Lewis

Where do abominable snowmen live?
In Chile!
Alex Cottee

What did the ghost teacher say to her pupils?
Watch the board while I go through it again!
Jemma Lynch

What do you write on a robot's gravestone?
Rust in peace!
Warick Falconer

What do you call a female ghoul on a plane?
An air ghostess!
Duncan McInnes

Why did the wizard turn his socks into music sheets?
Because his feet started to hum!
Natalie Sear

Why did the skeleton go to the Chinese restaurant?
To get some spare ribs!
Kayleigh Aubrey

How do you make a skeleton laugh?
Tickle his funny bone!
Penelope Jeffcock

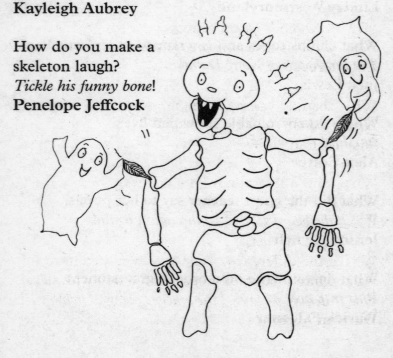

1st BOY: I got this haunted bike today.
2nd BOY: How do you know it's haunted?
1st BOY: Because it's got spooks on the wheels!
Hannah Davies

1st BOY: I keep dreaming about large red monsters with green teeth.
2nd BOY: Have you seen a doctor?
1st BOY: No, just large red monsters with green teeth!
Robert Parry

Why do witches fly on brooms?
Because vacuum cleaners are too heavy!
Luke Preece

What soap do vampires watch?
Horror-nation Street!
Aisha Khan

What kind of boat does Dracula use?
A blood vessel!
Bill French

What's the difference between a man who has walked into a haunted house, and a dog with fleas?
One is itching to go and the other is going to itch!
Duncan McInnes

There was a monster of Loch Ness,
Who was often seen in a dress.
The reporters asked why?
The monster replied,
'I wouldn't if I was photographed less.'
Kirstie Logan

What instrument does a skeleton play?
A trombone!
Jamie Curry

Where did Frankenstein's monster go to have his
head fitted to his shoulders?
Bolton!
Carl Manley

What do a footballer and a magician have in
common?
They both do hat tricks!
Saagar Patel

Have you been to the Himalayas?
Not yeti!
Joe Barthorpe

What do you call a ghost at a football match?
A spooktater!
Sean Hughes

What do you do when you see a skeleton dancing?
Jump out of your skin and join him!
Blair Grimley

What's the first thing a monster eats after having its tooth out?
The dentist!
Dawn Corney

What did the mummy ghost say to the baby ghost?
Spook when you're spooken to!
Christian Jones and Emma Brown

What is a monster's favourite football team?
Slitherpool!
Jessica Spooner

Why are skeletons always so calm?
Because nothing gets under their skin!
Liam Joynt

What do you get if you meet Dracula on the coldest night of the year?
Frostbite!
Lindzy Westmoreland

Why are monsters at home in the jungle?
Because it's full of creepers!
Daniel Edgerton

A boy was walking down the street when he saw a sea monster standing on the corner looking lost. The boy put a lead on the monster and took him to the police station. 'You should take him to the museum,' said the policeman. The next day the policeman saw the boy in the street, again with the sea monster on a lead. 'I thought I told you to take that monster to the museum,' said the policeman. 'I did' said the boy, 'and today, I'm taking him to the cinema!'
Gloria Hunniford

SCHOOL

TEACHER: If you had £2 in one jacket pocket and £2 in the other jacket pocket, what would you have?
PUPIL: Someone else's jacket, Miss!
Bob Holness, Ros Holness & Dougie Parker

A teacher brought her two parrots into class – one red and one green. They both flew out of an open window, and on to the branch of a tree. One of the pupils offered to go and fetch them. He came back with just the red parrot. 'I left the other one in the tree, Miss,' he said, 'because it's not ripe yet!'
Kieran Johnstone

TEACHER: If you have £6 and your dad gives you another £9, what would you have?
PUPIL: £6, Miss.
TEACHER: You don't know your arithmetic, boy.
PUPIL: You don't know my dad, Sir!
Rob Dixon

TEACHER: If you have five chocolate bars and your little brother asks for one, how many will you have left?
PUPIL: Five, of course!
Tanya Read

On a school outing, Alex ran out of money and borrowed £5 from his teacher. On the train back home he wanted a hamburger so he borrowed another £1 from his teacher, promising to give it back the next day. The next day Alex came into school clutching a squid that had a bandage around one of its tentacles. 'Here's the sick squid I owe you, Miss!' he said.

Alice Bradley

TEACHER: Name me two days of the week beginning with T.
PUPIL: Today and tomorrow, Miss!

Jack Maymon

'I've got a cousin with three feet,' said a boy to his teacher. 'How odd. How do you know?' asked the teacher. The boy replied 'Mum got a letter from her sister this morning, and she said that her eldest son had grown another foot during the last year!'

Tara Haycock

TEACHER: What's the most important thing to remember in a chemistry lesson?
PUPIL: Don't lick the spoon!

Louise Crawford

TEACHER: Give me a sentence with I in it.
PUPIL: I is…
TEACHER: No, always say 'I am'.
PUPIL: OK, I am the ninth letter of the alphabet!
Charles Jamieson

TEACHER: You should have been here at 9 o'clock.
PUPIL: Why, did something happen?
Gareth Lungley

TEACHER: For all those who were late this
morning because they stayed up to watch the
football, we're going to make the school more like a
football match. So you can all stay behind and do
extra time tonight, as a penalty!
Robert Wheatley

How do teachers dress in mid-January?
Quickly!
Lucy Purvis

TEACHER: Paul, why were you late this morning?
PAUL: Well Sir, I was dreaming about a football match and it was sudden death so I had to stay asleep!
Lauren Barker

TEACHER: Have you been stupid all your life?
PUPIL: Not yet, Miss!
Tom Portsmouth

TEACHER: How would you spell amphibian?
PUPIL: I wouldn't Miss, I'd write frog!
Natalie Owen

TEACHER: Now then, you're new here, aren't you. What's your name?

NEW PUPIL: Albert Mickey Jones, Miss.

TEACHER: I see. Can I call you Albert Jones then?

NEW PUPIL: My dad won't like that, Miss.

TEACHER: Why not?

NEW PUPIL: He doesn't like anyone taking the Mickey out of my name, Miss!

Sian Thomas

TEACHER: Melanie, you've been doing Sam's homework again. I recognise your writing in her book.

MELANIE: No, I haven't Miss. It's just we both used the same pencil!

Katie Firth

TEACHER: Why were you late for school this morning?

PUPIL: There are nine in our family, and the alarm was only set for eight!

Tania Price

What's the difference between a teacher and a train?
The teacher says, 'Spit out that gum,' and the train goes choo-choo!
Thomas Hurst

19

DANCE TEACHER: There are only two things stopping you from becoming the world's greatest ballerina.
STUDENT: What are they, Miss?
DANCE TEACHER: Your feet, dear!
Elin Roberts

TEACHER: What's your excuse for being late?
PUPIL: There was a notice on the bus saying 'Dogs must be carried', and I couldn't find one for ages!
Jack Davies

FIRST PUPIL: Why are you sitting in the gerbil's cage?
SECOND PUPIL: Because I want to be the teacher's pet!
Emily Wicks

Why did the boy take a car to school?
To drive his teacher up the wall!
Aisha Qureshi

What's the best way to cut down pollution in schools?
Use lead-free pencils!
Joshua Hartley

TEACHER: Can anybody tell me where elephants can be found?
PUPIL: Don't be silly Sir, they're much too big to lose!
Saffron Baxter

Why did the boy take a ladder to school?
Because it was a high school!
Amy Prosser

What's the best thing about going to school?
Coming home again!
Alice Troop

How can a teacher double his money?
By folding it in half!
Lucy Purvis

What are the two good things about being a teacher?
July and August!
Karl Phillips

TUESDAY

KNOCK KNOCK

Tuesday is Choose-Day! You can choose to have a giggle over Knock! Knock! jokes or Doctor! Doctor! jokes.

KNOCK! KNOCK!

Knock! Knock!
Who's there?
Amos.
Amos who?
A mosquito bit me!

Knock! Knock!
Who's there?
Andy.
Andy who?
Andy bit me again!
Alice Brunt

Knock! Knock!
Who's there?
Dummy.
Dummy who?
Dummy a favour and clear off!
Laura Nelson

Knock! Knock!
Who's there?
Consumption.
Consumption who?
Consumption not be done about your face?
Gemma Snodgrass

Knock! Knock!
Who's there?
Snow.
Snow who?
Snow use, I've forgotten my keys!
Simon Faulconbridge

Knock! Knock!
Who's there?
Giraffe.
Giraffe who?
Giraffe to sit next to me?
Evangeline Crossland

Knock! Knock!
Who's there?
Alex.
Alex who?
Alexplain later, if you let me in!
Rebecca Klys

Knock! Knock!
Who's there?
Marmalade.
Marmalade who?
Marmalade me a little egg!
Charlotte Troop

Knock! Knock!
Who's there?
Max.
Max who?
Max no difference, just open the door!
Alice Troop

Knock! Knock!
Who's there?
Stan.
Stan who?
Stan' back, I'm coming in!
Shayne Lattimer

Knock! Knock!
Who's there?
Jester.
Jester who?
Jester minute, I've forgotten!
Stacey Rowley

Knock! Knock!
Who's there?
Arthur.
Arthur who?
Arthur any cookies left?
Kieran Furnival

Knock! Knock!
Who's there?
Egbert.
Egbert who?
Egbert no bacon!
Sidney Higgins

Knock! Knock!
Who's there?
Police.
Police who?
Police may I come in?
Chris Drew

Knock! Knock!
Who's there?
Tuna.
Tuna who?
Tuna violin and it will
sound much better!
Bryn Robert Turnbull

Knock! Knock!
Who's there?
Hatch.
Hatch who?
That's a bad cold you've got!
Terri Morris

Knock! Knock!
Who's there?
Irish Stew.
Irish Stew who?
Irish stew in the name of the law!
Richard Maddocks

Knock! Knock!
Who's there?
Jim.
Jim who?
Jim mind if I stay here tonight?
Tom Portsmouth

Knock! Knock!
Who's there?
Harry.
Harry who?
Harry up and open this door!
Aisha Khan

Knock! Knock!
Who's there?
Noah.
Noah who?
Noah good chip shop – I'm hungry!
Natasha Fisher

Knock! Knock!
Who's there?
Alison.
Alison who?
Alison to my radio every morning!
Abigail Purser

Knock! Knock!
Who's there?
Wendy.
Wendy who?
Wendyou think you can open this door?
Rebecca Bird

Knock! Knock!
Who's there?
Owl.
Owl who?
Owl you know, if you don't open the door?
Rachel Hutchinson

★ ★ ★ ★ ★ ★ ★

DOCTOR! DOCTOR!

Doctor! Doctor! I think I'm a bee.
Buzz off, then!
Ashley Baker

Doctor! Doctor! I still feel sick.
Did you drink your medicine after your bath?
No, I was too full after drinking the bath!
Andrea Glen

Doctor! Doctor! I feel like a pair of curtains.
Well pull yourself together then!
Carl Smith

Doctor! Doctor! I've swallowed my camera film.
Well, let's hope nothing develops!
Sarah Waechtler

Doctor! Doctor! I think I'm a goat.
How long have you felt like this?
Since I was a kid!
Tommy Hindmarsh

Doctor! Doctor! I feel like a pack of cards.
Sit over there, I'll deal with you later!
Lauren Croft

Doctor! Doctor! I think I need glasses.
I think you're right, this is a pet shop!
Daniel English

Doctor! Doctor! I keep thinking I'm a dog.
Take a seat then.
I can't, I'm not allowed on the cushions!
Tom Portsmouth

A man walked into a doctor's surgery with a parrot
on his head. 'How can I help you?' asked the
doctor. 'You can get this stupid man off my feet!'
replied the parrot.
Kirsty Doran

Doctor! Doctor! Every time I drink a cup of tea, I get a terrible pain in my eye.
Have you tried taking the spoon out of the cup?
Aimee Paton

Doctor! Doctor! I feel like a bell.
Give me a ring when you're feeling better!
Charlotte Troop

Doctor! Doctor! I suffer with a lot of wind. Do you have anything for it?
Certainly Sir, here's a kite!
Jack Lewis

Doctor! Doctor! I'm shrinking.
Well, you'll just have to be a little patient!
Michaela Drummond

Doctor! Doctor! I feel like a dustbin.
Stop talking rubbish!
Liam Gaughan

When Mary had a little lamb,
The doctor was surprised.
But when Old MacDonald had a farm,
He could hardly believe his eyes!
Kirstie Logan

Doctor! Doctor! A crab just bit my toe.
Which one?
I don't know, all crabs look alike to me!
Richard Gwyn Jones

Doctor! Doctor! I feel like an apple.
Don't worry, I won't bite!
Stacie Donnelly

Doctor! Doctor! I've lost my memory.
When did this happen?
When did what happen?
Saagar Patel

Doctor! Doctor! Can you help me out?
Certainly Sir, it's the same way you came in!
Daniel Carney

A man went to the doctor with a badly injured toe. The nurse directed him to the next room, and told him to remove his clothes. 'But I only hurt my toe,' complained the man. 'Why do I need to take my clothes off?' The nurse replied 'Everyone who sees the doctor has to undress. It's our policy.' 'Well,' said the man, 'I think it's a stupid policy! Making me undress just to look at my toe.' From the next room, another man's voice piped in, 'That's nothing, I just came to fix the telephone!'
Paul Brown

WEDNESDAY

Wednesday is When?day
(Who? What? Why? and How?day too!)
so here are lots of question and answer jokes.

First some questions without answers:

Why don't sheep shrink when it rains?
What was the best thing before sliced bread?
Don't you find it worrying that a doctor works in a
Practice?
If a turtle has no shell, is he homeless, or naked?
Matthew Kelly

And why can't you have:
A chocolate toaster?
An inflatable dartboard?
A solar-powered torch?
J Glen

33

or
An underwater hairdryer?
Windscreen wipers on a submarine?
Siobhan Fitzpatrick

Did you hear about the magician who walked down
the road and turned into a shop?
Simeon Courtie

And now lots of questions with answers!

On what day was Luke Skywalker born?
May the 4th! (be with you)
Frances White

What did the lady's bra say to the top hat?
You go on ahead, I'll give these two a lift!
June Whitfield

Why did the viper vipe 'er nose?
Because the adder 'ad 'er 'ankerchief!
Simeon Courtie

Can February March?
No, but April May!
Rebecca Klys

What's green and goes camping?
A boy sprout!
John Hoare

Why did Robin Hood steal from the rich?
Because the poor had nothing worth taking!
Kirsty Moore

What do you call someone who used to like
tractors, but doesn't any more?
An extractor fan!
Daniel Hall

Why did the undertaker chop up all the bodies?
So they could rest in pieces!
Jessica Spooner

What do you call a Tellytubby who's been robbed?
Tubby!
Jason Hawcutt

What happens when the Queen burps?
She issues a royal pardon!
Charlotte Troop

How do you get rid of varnish?
Take away the R!
Rosie Whitehorn

Why do people laugh up their sleeves?
Because that's where their funny bone is!
Jake Whitehorn

What do you call well repaired socks?
Darned good!
Conor McBride

What does a doctor say when he X-rays a teddy bear?
Stuffin' to worry about!
Graham Thorpe

Why is a football stadium so cool?
Because it's full of fans!
Patrick Daly

Why shouldn't you dress in front of a Pokémon?
Because he'll pik-a-chu!
Georgina Oliver

What does a dentist call his X-rays?
Tooth pics!
Sally-Ann Burden

What are German cars made of?
Polos!
Andrew MacLeod

How many ears does Mr Spock have?
Three – the left ear, the right ear and the final front ear!
Robert Kelly

What would you do if Pikachu's eyes fell off?
Poke'em on!
Laurence Kelly

What has four eyes and can't see?
Mississippi!
Shenaz Souter

What trees walk around in twos?
Pear trees!
Andrea Obremski

What do you call a fairy that hasn't washed?
Stinker Bell!
William Kilgore

Why was Cinderella so bad at football?
Because her coach was a pumpkin, and she ran away from the ball!
Rachel Lambert

What happens when you dial 666?
The police come upside down!
Chloë Rai

How does a plant find its way to the garden?
It asks for the root!
Zoë Podmore

Why do we plant bulbs in the garden?
So the worms can see where they're going!
Piers Lee

What do you do if the M6 is closed?
Drive up the M3 twice!
Michael Peter Beattie

What is the worst weather for an archer?
Mist!
Andrew Cunningham

What did the puddle say to the rain?
You can drop in any time!
Charlie Roberts

How do you make a tissue dance?
Put a little boogie into it!
Laura Codlin

What do you get if your head is chopped off?
A splitting headache!
Jessica Spooner

Why do traffic wardens have yellow bands around
their hats?
So people don't park on their heads!
Charlotte Troop

What do you call a jogger in a safari park?
Fast food!
Jack Lewis

What's black and white and noisy?
A penguin playing a drum!
Steve Drake

How do you get 1000 Pikachus on a bus?
Pokémon!
Stella Paskins

Why did the belt go to jail?
Because it was holding some trousers up!
Alex Cottee

What's small, hairy and has 6 legs?
An ant in a fur coat!
Kieran Johnstone

What do you get when you eat Christmas decorations?
Tinsel-itis!
Thomas Digney

What does Luke Skywalker shave with?
A laser blade!
Liam Joynt

What grows bigger the more you take from it?
A hole!
Patrick Daly

What starts with an 'e', ends with an 'e' and only has one letter?
An envelope!
Jacqueline Tilly

Why did the golfer bring two pairs of trousers?
In case he got a hole in one!
Alison Adams

What illness did everyone catch on the Starship
Enterprise?
Chicken spocks!
Liam Joynt

How long is a minute?
Depends which side of the bathroom door you're on!
Alison Adams

Who invented fire?
Some bright spark!
Gemma Smith

What do you get if you cross a crocodile with a
maths teacher?
Snappy answers!
Kirsty Francis

What did one stereo system say to the other?
Hi Fi!
Andrea Obremski

What do you get if you cross a giraffe and a hedgehog?
A very long toothbrush!
Sophie Barfield

What do you get if you cross a wizard with an iceberg?
A cold spell!
Nicola Wood

Why can't you play cards in the jungle?
Because there are too many cheetahs!
Scott Chapman

What do you call a greenfly with no eyes, no legs and no wings?
A bogey!
Jake McDonnell

What do you call a radio presenter who plays records in alphabetical order?
An ABCDJ!
Stefan Edwards

Who's in charge of the tissue factory?
The Hanky Chief!
Bradley Bosher

What do you call a clever boy with sweets in his pocket?
Smartie-pants!
Clare Samson

How many jugglers does it take to change a lightbulb?
Only one, but it takes at least 3 lightbulbs!
Lisa Bird

Why was the Ancient Egyptian girl worried?
Because her Daddy was a Mummy!
Richard Southern

Why are England and a 3-pin plug the same?
They're both rubbish in Europe!
Jamie Creus

What do you call two robbers?
A pair of nickers!
Kate Johnson

What goes 'ha ha ha plop'?
A man laughing his head off!
Steven Shing

Why can't cars play football?
Because they've only got one boot!
James Gillett

What happened to the girl who slept with her head under her pillow?
The tooth fairy took away all her teeth!
Cheryl Hughes

What goes 'dot dot dot croak'?
A morse toad!
James Paramore

There were two teddy bears in the airing cupboard.
Which was the one in the Army?
The one on the tank!
Toni Prince

Who was the first man on the moon?
A spaceman!
Heidi Ditchmouth

Why is 'E' lazy?
Because it's always in bed!
Philip Webster

Where can you dance in California?
In San Fran-disco!
Stephanie Thomas

Which Dutch city is covered in sticky sweet stuff?
Amster-jam!
Kayleigh Hughes

What do you call a crazy spaceman?
An astro-nut!
Jamie West

Where was the Queen crowned?
On her head!
Natalie Owen

What's green and square?
An orange in disguise!
Trudi Stott

Why did the football coach give his team lighters?
Because they kept losing their matches!
Ceri Lloyd

What colour is the wind?
Blew!
Tanya Prince

Why was the boxer called Rembrandt?
Because he was always on the canvas!
Anthony Kennedy

Why are babies good at football?
Because they're great dribblers!
Victoria McKeown

Who invented King Arthur's round table?
Sir Cumference!
Andrew Fish

Which member of a cricket team wears the biggest hat?
The one with the biggest head!
Aisha Khan

What does it say on the door of a pharoah's tomb?
Toot'n come in!
Helen Cinnamond

How do you keep an idiot waiting?
I'll tell you tomorrow!
Daniel Hall

What do you call university students on the underground?
A tube of smarties!
Natalie Bailey

Did you hear about the karate champion who joined the army?
The first time he saluted, he nearly killed himself!
Seren Evans

What's a volcano?
A mountain with hiccups!
Natalie York

How many children does it take to do the washing- up?
Three — one to wash, one to dry and one to pick up the pieces!
Vicky Bilton

Why does Mr Potato Head not go to fancy restaurants?
Because it costs him an arm and a leg!
Michael McLaren

Why did the ship made from butter sink?
Because the Anchor fell through the Flora!
Brendon Carr

What goes '99 plonk, 99 plonk'?
A centipede with a wooden leg!
Zara Glenn

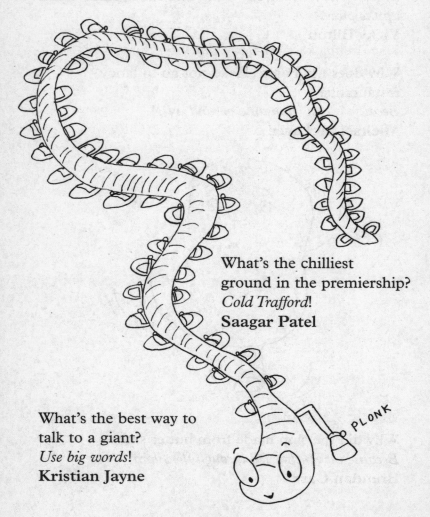

What's the chilliest
ground in the premiership?
Cold Trafford!
Saagar Patel

What's the best way to
talk to a giant?
Use big words!
Kristian Jayne

What do you have to take the top off to put the bottom on?
A toilet seat!
Mark Summerscales

Why do goalkeepers have a lot of money?
Because they are good savers!
Joseph Quinney

Why was Humpty Dumpty a disappointment?
He wasn't all he was cracked up to be!
Rebecca Telford

Why couldn't the sailors play cards?
Because the captain was standing on the deck!
Saffron Baxter

What do you get if you cross a group of stars with a silver cup?
A constellation prize!
Laura O'Rahilly

Why is the sky so high?
So the birds don't bump their heads!
Megan McCann

What do you call a snowman with a suntan?
A puddle!
Iram Rasool

What magazine does a clock read?
The Times!
Alistair Laycock

Why did the fire switch off?
Because it had a slight temperature!
Nicholas Miltiadous

Why did the jellybean go to school?
Because he wanted to be a Smartie!
Andrew Sullman

What award did the inventor of the
door-knocker win?
The no-bell prize!
Daniel Holmes

And finally for this question and answer session:

While on a visit to Russia, I asked Boris Yeltsin to
describe the state of Russia at that time. 'Good,' he
replied. I said, 'Would you like to give a more in-
depth view?' He paused, then said, 'Very good.'
John Major

Roberto! Anna!

THURSDAY

Sherlock Foams!

Bob!

Thursday is Thor's day — named after the god of war. So Thursday's jokes are all about names, starting with one about Thor himself!

The God of War rode into town
Upon a handsome filly,
'I'm Thor,' he cried,
The horse replied,
'You forgot your thaddle, thilly!'
Amy Prosser

What do you call an Italian with a rubber toe?
Roberto!
Jonny Searle

What do you call Bob the Builder when he retires?
Bob!
Steve Drake

Who designed the first rain jacket?
Anna Rack!
Debbie Maguire

What do you call a woman playing pool with a
crate of beer on her head?
Beer-tricks Potter!
Michael Podmore

What do you call a detective in the bath?
Sherlock Foams!
Shayne Lattimer

What do you call a nun with
a washing machine on her head?
Systematic!
Thomas Digney

What do you call a man who stops a river?
Adam!
Joshua Judge

What do you call a man sitting on the carpet?
Matt!
Jonathan McKie

What do you call a man with leaves in his trousers?
Russell!
Aaron Penn

What do you call a man who's black and blue all over?
Bruce!
Laura Mathie

Which football player keeps up the fuel supply?
Paul Gas Coin!
Saagar Patel

What has 8 guns and terrorises the ocean?
Billy the Squid!
Andrew Moss

What do you call a lady on the horizon?
Dot!
A J Nisbet

What do you call a lady with two toilet seats on her head?
Lulu!
April Finan

What do you call a man with a spade on his head?
Doug!
Dani Morris

And there were several jokes sent in about a girl called Mary! Here are two of them:

Mary had a little lamb.
Peter had a pup.
Chrissy had a crocodile,
That ate the others up.
Amy Perry

Mary had a little lamb.
She ate it with mint sauce.
Now everywhere that Mary goes,
The lamb goes too, of course!
Tomos Edwards

Friday's jokes have to be
about food. There are also loads of Waiter! Waiter!
jokes in this section, in case you are feeling hungry!

What's the best day to eat eggs and bacon?
Fry day!
Alexis Harbot

Why did the orange have to go to hospital?
Because it wasn't peeling very well!
Sarah Salisbury

What did the grape say when the elephant sat on it?
Nothing, it just gave a little wine!
Liam Joynt

What jumps and makes you cry?
A spring onion!
Gemma Wray

Did you hear about the fight in the biscuit tin?
The Bandit hit the Twix over the head with a Club and escaped in a Taxi!
Craig Lyttle

Two crisps were walking down the road. A car pulled up and the driver said, 'Would you like a lift?' 'No thanks,' the crisps replied, 'we're Walkers!'
Sophie Griffiths

Why did the biscuit cry?
His mum was a wafer too long!
Why did the biscuit cry again?
Someone dunked his dad in a cup of tea!
Michael Spence

A peanut sitting on a railway track,
His heart is all a-flutter.
The train comes whistling round the bend,
Toot toot – peanut butter!
Emma Ternell

What's the fastest cake in the world?
Scone!
Ashley Baker

A couple of builders were working on the roof of the local curry house. One fell through the roof and is now in hospital in a korma!
Daniel Taylor

What sits in custard looking cross?
Apple grumble!
Amy Prosser

What do Jelly Babies wear in the rain?
Gum boots!
Kirsty Moore

What is rhubarb?
Embarrassed celery!
Chelsea Avey

Why didn't the strawberry drive?
Because it didn't want to be in a jam!
Jack Lewis

A man walks into a bar and asks, 'Have you got any helicopter crisps?' The barmaid replies, 'No we only have plain crisps here!'
Jenny Pointon

Who swings from cake to cake?
Tarzipan!
Daniel Robinson

How do elves get indigestion?
By goblin their food!
Sally-Ann Burden

Why was the chef angry?
Because he had a big chip on his shoulder!
Warick Falconer

Which vegetable is the most impatient?
A queue-cumber!
Liam Vaughan

What kind of shoes can you make out of banana
skins?
Slippers!
Oliver Court

What is bread?
Raw toast!
Joseph Blewitt

How do monkeys toast bread?
They put it under the gorilla!
Kayleigh Hughes

How do mushrooms count?
On their fungus!
Natalie Owen

What's the difference between a fish and a piano?
You can tune a piano, but you can't tuna fish!
Katy Woodward

A ham sandwich walked into a bar and said to the
barman, 'A pint of beer, please.' The barman
replied, 'I'm sorry, we don't serve food!'
Steven Fletcher

What's the difference between a brussels sprout and
a bogey?
You can't get a kid to eat a brussels sprout!
Alex Johnston

What's the difference between an elephant and
peanut butter?
An elephant doesn't stick to the roof of your mouth!
Lisa Williams

What do you get if you cross a hedgehog with a
giraffe?
A very long toothbrush!
Kimberley Waechtler

What's the difference between a policeman and a
soldier?
You can't dip a policeman in your egg!
Alexander Foulds

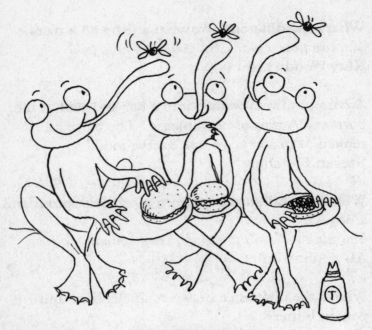

What do frogs eat with their hamburgers?
French flies!
Feifei Yuan

What is a meatball?
A dance in a butcher's shop!
Natalie Bailey

Why do bananas wear suntan lotion?
Because they peel easily!
Carly Louise Hurne

What do vegetarian vicars say before meals?
Lettuce pray!
Briony de Vera-Lee

Why aren't footballers ever asked to dinner?
Because they're always dribbling!
Sean Bartlett

Why were the naughty eggs sent out of the class?
Because they kept playing practical yolks!
Max Crew-Gee

Why was the banana so good at PE?
It could do the banana-splits!
Kira Siddens

How many eggs does it take to make a stink bomb?
A phew!
Rebecca Telford

What cheese is made backwards?
Edam!
Liam Joynt

What comes from grapes and is highly explosive?
Wine-amite!
Amy Whyte

Two men were wandering in the desert. One man was tired, so he sat down. He asked his friend to bring him a piece of bacon from the bacon tree that he could see. The other man did as he was told but came back quickly, covered in cuts and bruises. 'That wasn't a bacon tree you saw,' he said. 'It was a hambush!'
Alice Brunt

'Waiter! Waiter! Get me a crocodile sandwich – and make it snappy!'
Bob Holness, Ros Holness & Dougie Parker

Waiter! Waiter! Is this tea or coffee? It tastes like vinegar!
In that case Sir, it's tea. The coffee tastes like petrol!
Alice Troop

Waiter! Waiter! There's a fly in my custard.
I'll fetch him a spoon, Sir!
Thomas Askew

Waiter! Waiter! There's a fly in my soup.
Throw him a doughnut – they make great life belts!
Fern Elliot

Waiter! Waiter!
Why are you carrying
a tray of candles and bulbs?
I'm serving a light lunch, Sir!
Lindzy Westmoreland

Two men suffering from amnesia were sitting on a beach. One said he was going to get an ice-cream. The other asked if he would get him an ice-cream too. The first man said he would. His friend added, 'With a chocolate flake, please, and hundreds and thousands, and chocolate sauce.' 'OK,' said the first man. Five minutes later he was back. 'Here are your chips,' he said. 'You idiot,' said his friend, 'You forgot the pie!'
Shellyfaye Lahf

Waiter! Waiter! Have you got frog's legs?
No Sir, it's just the way I walk!
Rebecca Veasey

Waiter! Waiter! There's a flea in my soup.
Tell him to hop it!
Thomas Askew

Waiter! Waiter! There's a frog in my soup.
I'm sorry Sir, the fly is on holiday!
Charlotte Nicholls

Waiter! Waiter! There's a spider drowning in my soup!
It hardly looks deep enough to drown in, Sir!
Scott Crouch

A tramp knocked on the door asking for food. The woman who answered the door asked if he liked cold rice pudding. The tramp nodded. The woman responded, 'Well, come back tomorrow then, when it's cooled down!'
Craig West

What do you get if you cross a Spice Girl with a takeaway?
Egg fried spice!
Richard McCourt

A man bought a Thermos flask because he was told it would keep hot things hot and cold things cold. Next day, at work, the man's colleagues asked him what was in his Thermos flask. He replied, 'Two choc ices and a Cuppa Soup!'
Steven Fletcher

Waiter, can you explain why there are footprints on the food you've just brought me?
Yes Sir. You rushed in, asked for a large omelette and told me to step on it!
Dewi Jones

What do you get if you cross old potatoes with lumpy mince?
School dinners!
Lucy Purvis

What do you get if you cross peanut butter and a quilt?
A bread spread!
Shayne Lattimer

What do you get if you cross a jelly with a sheepdog?
Collie-wobbles!
Aimee Plunkett

What do you get if you cross a cat and a lemon?
A sour puss!
Laura Codlin

How can you tell if an elephant has been in the fridge?
There are footprints in the butter!
James Gething-Lewis

Hooray — it's the weekend! Saturday is a time you can be with your family, so Saturday's jokes are about Families and... there's a section of Favourites too!

Families

HUSBAND: I saved us money today. I ran home behind the bus.
WIFE: You stupid creature, you'd have saved us a lot more if you'd run behind a taxi!
Vivien Creegor

GIRL: Mummy, can I have a new pair of plimsolls for gym?
MUM: No, Jim will have to buy his own!
Sian Edwards

Grandad was trying to do a jigsaw puzzle but finding it difficult so he rang his grandson for help. The grandson arrived and asked, 'What's it supposed to be, Grandad?' 'A red chicken,' replied Grandad. The boy looked at the box. 'Grandad,' he said, 'put the cornflakes back in the box!'
Faye Sharman

MOTHER: Darling, I'm really busy, can you change your little sister?
DAUGHTER: Why? Has she worn out already?
Kieran Johnstone

BROTHER: I can lift an elephant with one hand.
SISTER: Now you're boasting.
BROTHER: OK, find me an elephant with one hand and I'll lift it!
Charles Crossland

GIRL: Daddy, there's a man with a beard at the door.
DADDY: Tell him I've got one already!
Charles Fry

GIRL: I'm homesick.
MOTHER: But this is your home.
GIRL: I know, I'm sick of it!
Craig Hackett

DAD: Don't jump off that board! There's no water in the pool.
SON: That's OK, Dad, I can't swim yet!
Jonathan Baxter

My little brother is so thin that when we go to the park, the ducks throw bread at him!
Jack Lewis

SISTER: Last night I had to close the door in my nightie.
BROTHER: That's a funny place to have a door!
Sabrina Wellard

MUM: What did your father say about your school report?
SON: Shall I leave out the bad language?
MUM: Yes of course, dear.
SON: He didn't say anything, Mum!
Kirsty Francis

HUSBAND: Why are you going around telling everyone I'm an idiot?
WIFE: I'm sorry, is it supposed to be a secret?
Rebecca Telford

MUM: Have you given the goldfish fresh water yet?
SON: No, they haven't drunk the water I gave them last week yet!
Saffron Baxter

DAD: How are your marks at school?
SON: They're underwater.
DAD: What?
SON: They're below C!
Laura O'Rahilly

FATHER: What's on the telly tonight, Son?
SON: Same as always, Dad, a vase of flowers and a picture of Grandma!
Kirsty Francis

MUM: How is school? You're not still messing about are you?

BOY: School's fine. I'm still kept as centre forward in football and I'm still right back in lessons!

Divya Jani

FIRST ANGEL: What do you think the weather will be like tomorrow?

SECOND ANGEL: I think it will be cloudy.

FIRST ANGEL: Thank goodness for that. We can sit down at last!

Kieran Johnstone

Favourites

What is a boxer's favourite drink?
Punch!
Shayne Lattimer

What's a crocodile's favourite card game?
Snap!
Aaron Campbell

Who is a penguin's favourite aunt?
Aunt-arctica!
Harry Cox

What's a teddy bear's favourite pasta?
Tagliateddy!
Saagar Patel

What's a vampire's favourite dessert?
Leaches and scream!
Charlotte Blom

What's a penguin's favourite pudding?
Baked Alaska!
Charlotte Wadey

What is a sheep's favourite game?
Baa-dminton!
Warick Falconer

What is a bird's favourite breakfast?
Tweet-a-bix!
Aimee Plunkett

What is a frog's favourite sweet?
Lolli-hops!
Michael Peter Beattie

What is a cat's favourite holiday resort?
The Canary Islands!
Andrew Moss

What's a cowardly man's favourite beer?
Courage!
Adam Tyndall

What's a hedgehog's favourite food?
Prickled onions!
Adam Tyndall

What's a squirrel's favourite chocolate?
Whole nut!
Max Crew-Gee

What's a cow's favourite breakfast?
Moo-sli!
Robert Hobin

What's a ghost's favourite food?
Spooketti!
Emma Woodbridge

What is a monkey's favourite flower?
Chimp-pansies!
Chelsea Hilton

What's a plumber's favourite vegetable?
A leek!
Lindzy Westmoreland

What is Dr Jekyll's favourite game?
Hyde and seek!
Chloë Rai

What is a hen's favourite TV programme?
That's Hentertainment!
Naomi McFaul

What is Scooby-Doo's favourite watersport?
Scooby diving, of course!
Laura Bryers

So many of you sent in Animal jokes, that we have devoted the whole of Sunday to them. With no school and the shopping done, you should have plenty of time for looking after your animals... and for giggling!

What do you call a dinosaur with only one eye?
A doyouthinkhesawus!
Bob Holness, Ros Holness & Dougie Parker

What happened to the cat that ate the wool?
She had mittens!
Jack Lewis

What's the correct name for a water otter?
A kettle!
Christopher Hall

What travels at 60mph under water?
A motor pike and side carp!
Thomas Digney

How do you get four elephants in a Ka?
Two in the back and two in the front!
How do you get four giraffes in a Ka?
You can't, it's full of elephants!
Lhia and Jared Forde

What do you call a septic cat?
Puss!
Eliza Brodie

How do you stop a polar bear charging?
Take away its credit card!
Fiona Rowley

What's green and sits in the corner?
A naughty frog!
Lillie Christie

Where do bees go to the toilet?
At a BP station!
Oliver Atack

What do you call a camel with three humps?
Humphrey!
Vincent Crossland

Why do tigers eat raw meat?
Because no one taught them how to cook!
Debbie Maguire

How do you stop a fish from smelling?
Hold its nose!
J Glen

How do you get 5 donkeys on a fire engine?
*Two in the front, two in the back and one on top going
'EE AW, EE AW, EE AW!'*
Aaron Leckey

What is the biggest moth?
A mam-moth!
Gemma Smith

Two polar bears were having lunch. The little polar
bear said to the big polar bear, 'Can I have a Kit-
Kat?' The big polar bear replied, 'Don't be greedy,
you haven't finished your penguin yet!'
Sarah Hill

What do you call a fish with no eyes?
A fsh!
Elisabeth Macey

What do you call a woodpecker with no beak?
A head banger!
Maria Parkins

What do you call a tail-less glow worm?
De-lighted!
Charlotte Armstrong

Why do spiders like the Internet?
Because of all the websites!
John O'Hara

What do you get if you put a cow on a seesaw?
Milkshake!
Michael Spence

What do you call elephants without trunks?
Nudists!
Harry Winteringham

How do you catch a squirrel?
Climb a tree and act like a nut!
Jack Wilkinson

Did you hear about the stupid woodworm?
He was found in a rock!
James Kelly

A snail went into a pub and asked for a pint of
lager. The barman picked him up and threw him
out. Twenty years later the snail returned and
asked, 'What did you do that for?'
Ben Handley

Two elephants walk off a cliff. Boom, Boom!
Luke Storey

What did the chick say when his mum laid an orange egg?
Look what marma-laid!
Rebecca Telford

What is the main ingredient in dog biscuits?
Collie flour!
Sam Hughes

Where would you find a prehistoric cow?
In a moo-seum!
Bibi Smith

How does a pig get to hospital?
In a hambulance!
Leonie Hutton

1st MAN: Have you ever seen an elephant hiding behind a flower?
2nd MAN: No.
1st MAN: Good at it, aren't they!
Vikki Emberson

What did the hedgehog say to the other hedgehog before he crossed the road?
I don't think I'll bother – look what happened to the zebra!
Lynn Hamilton

Why did the cockerel cross the road?
To show his girlfriend he wasn't chicken!
Aneurin Pomphrey

What did the farmer say to his flying sheepdog?
Land Rover!
Kyle Taylor

What lays eggs with funny yolks?
A comedi-hen!
Charlotte Troop

What medicine do you give a sick ant?
Antibiotics!
Lindzy Westmoreland

What dog hides from the frying pan?
A sausage dog!
Alice Troop

What's green, slimy and goes 'hith'?
A snake with a lisp!
Ben Whitehorn

What do you call a pig with an itch?
Pork scratching!
Conor McBride

Why does a giraffe eat so little?
Because a little goes a long way!
Kieran Johnstone

What do you call a travelling flea?
An itch hiker!
Thomas Digney

1st BOY: My brother named his stick insect Buzz.
2nd BOY: Why?
1st BOY: Because it isn't Woody!
Rob Dixon

What lives in the sea and attacks other fish?
Jack the Kipper!
Sally-Ann Burden

Why can't 101 dalmatians play hide-and-seek?
Because they'd get spotted!
Siobhan Fitzpatrick

What do you call a mermaid without a boyfriend?
Single fish!
Greig McCachlan and Andrew McKendrick

What do you call a dog on a pogo stick?
A Springer!
Andrea Obremski

What do penguins drive?
Arcticulated trucks!
Charlotte Wadey

How do you know if an elephant is under your bed?
Your nose hits the ceiling!
Shayne Lattimer

What's the difference between an Indian elephant
and an African elephant?
About 3000 miles!
Hannah Farebrother

How does a lion pray?
With its paws together!
Zoë Podmore

Why don't gorillas eat Smarties?
Because they're too hard to peel!
Pippa Gartrell

Why are some fish at the bottom of the sea?
Because they dropped out of school!
Charlotte Wadey

What animal would be useful as a bed?
A lion!
Clare Samson

What is a snail?
A slug with a crash helmet!
Lucy Purvis

What do you call 500 penguins in Leicester Square?
Lost!
Sophie Newcombe

Which birds can lift the heaviest weight?
Cranes!
Aimee Plunkett

How do you know if a hippo is sitting next to you?
He has an H on his pencil case!
Natalie Owen

What do you call a snake that wants to be a bird?
A feather boa!
Lauren Still

Why are goldfish orange?
Because the water makes them rusty!
Elen Thomas

Why do penguins carry fish in their beaks?
Because they don't have any pockets!
Carys Jones

Why do rhinos drink so much water?
Because they don't like tea or coffee!
Christopher Cleverley

What do you get if you cross a fly and an elephant?
An overweight spider!
Natalie Owen

1st COW: Have you heard about this mad cow disease?
2nd COW: *Don't ask me, I'm a helicopter*!
David Jones

Where would you find a tortoise with no legs?
Where you left it!
Jamie Adams

Which country do goldfish come from?
Finland!
Martin Venning

What's the biggest mouse in the world?
A hippopota-mouse!
Ceri Lloyd

How can you tell which end of a worm is its head?
Tickle its middle and see which end laughs!
Tanya Prince

What did the beaver say to the tree?
It's been nice gnawing you!
Aisha Khan

What did the duck say to the shopkeeper?
Put it on my bill, please!
Kayleigh Row

What does Cinderella's pet penguin wear?
Glass flippers!
Scott Pargetor

When is it bad to have a black cat following you?
When you're a mouse!
Thor Wyles

What do you call a fish on a frozen lake?
An ice-skate!
Julia Hosken

There were two fish in a tank. One said to the
other, 'Do you know how to drive this thing?'
Colin Houston

There were two cows in a field. One said, 'Moo'.
The other said, 'Hey, I was going to say that!'
Nicola Feltham

Twenty-two ants were playing football in a saucer.
One ant says to the other, 'We must play better
than this tomorrow – we're playing in the cup!'
Roxy Lyne

What sort of tiles can't you stick to a wall?
Reptiles!
Michael and Rebecca Gardner

A daredevil fly was hit by a car. The fly became a ghost and said to his friends, 'I'd do that again, if I had the guts!'.
Sebastian Toy

Why do ducks have flat feet?
To stomp out forest fires!
Why do elephants have flat feet?
To stomp out burning ducks!
Jordan Collin

What do you get if you cross a snake with a kangaroo?
A jump rope!
Gemma Ramsey

What's a snake's favourite lesson?
Hiss-tory!
Laura Bunting

"ANYDAY"

Monday Tuesday Wednesday Thursday Friday

Otherwise known as the STOP PRESS jokes –
late arrivals from the 2001 Child Of Achievement™
Award Winners!

What's the difference between unlawful and illegal?
Unlawful is against the law, illegal is a sick bird!
Matthew Moore

LUCY: Dad, there's a man at the door collecting
for a swimming pool.
DAD: *Give him a glass of water, then*!
Joseph Atack

How does a ghost address his letters?
Tomb it may concern!
Kaylee Davidson

What did the father ghost say to the baby ghost?
Fasten your sheet belts!
Rehman Gova

OPTICIAN: Have your eyes ever been checked?
CUSTOMER: No, they've always been blue!
Christopher Ashton

Knock! Knock!
Who's there?
Lucy.
Lucy who?
Lucylastic can let you down!
Laura Buxton

Knock! Knock!
Who's there?
Daisy.
Daisy who?
Daisy works, nights he sleeps!
Hannah Barker

What do you call a man with a number plate on
his head?
Reg!
What do you call a dead man with a number plate
on his head?
X-Reg!
Rosie Jones

Who is a scary man who is too soft?
Peter Cushion!
Craig Acton

Why does the capital city of Ireland grow so fast?
Because it keeps Dublin!
Patrick O'Brien

What's orange and sounds like a parrot?
A carrot!
Thomas Rowson

What's yellow and white and travels at 100mph?
A train driver's egg sandwich!
George Page

A man went to a fancy-dress party with a woman
on his back. The host asked him what he had come
as, and he replied 'A ninja turtle.' The host pointed
to the woman on his back and asked 'What's that
then?' and he replied, 'It's Michelle!'
Dominic Hanley

Why don't your handkerchief and your nose like
each other?
Because they always come to blows when they meet!
Rebecca Marshman

What bird never sings?
A ladybird!
Kirsty Ashton

Waiter! Waiter! Do you do takeaways?
Yes sir, six take away two is four!
James Studley

TEACHER: Does anyone need help with spelling?
PUPIL: Yes, Sir. How do you spell R S P C A?
Julie Ahmed

TEACHER: I asked you to draw a picture of a cow
eating grass. Why have you handed in a blank piece
of paper?
PUPIL: Because the cow ate all the grass, so that's
why there's no grass in the picture.
TEACHER: But where's the cow?
PUPIL: There's no point in the cow hanging
around, when there's no grass to eat, is there?
Kirsty Roberts

A tomato and a hat were having a race. The tomato
said to the hat, 'You go on ahead and I'll ketchup!'
Jagjit Singh Chuk

SUMO WRESTLER: (Getting off bus) This bus was very slow.
CONDUCTOR: It'll pick up now you're getting off!
Jonathan White

At a bus stop the other day I saw a man with one glove on. I asked him why he only wore one glove and he said that the weather forecast this morning had said it was going to be cold – but on the other hand, it might be warm!
Connor Hanley

A man went to stay in a hotel, and in the morning he asked the landlady for baked beans for breakfast. Later that day the landlady had a phone call to say the man had been taken ill and was in hospital. 'That's strange,' said the landlady, 'he was full of beans this morning!'
Harriot Bates

A man walks into a hardware store and asks, 'Can I have some nails, please?' The shopkeeper asked, 'How long do you want them?' The man replied, 'I'd like to keep them, please!'
Victoria Maughan

What is a cow's favourite planet?
The Mooooon!
Sean Barlow

What do you call spiders that have just got married?
*Newly web*s!
Kaylee Davidson

101 dalmatians have just cleaned Roger and Anita's kitchen.
How did it look?
Spotless!
Mark McFarlane

What was the name of the movie about a killer lion that swam under water?
Claws!
Connor McFarlane

Why didn't the worms go on to Noah's Ark in an apple?
*Because they had to go in pair*s!
Carlos Rodriguez

Where did Walt Disney find Donald Duck?
In a quacker!
Kevin Thompson

What is a millipede father's worst nightmare?
Buying his children shoes!
Holly Hynes

A flea jumped over the swinging doors of a saloon,
drank three whiskies and jumped out again. He
picked himself up, dusted himself down and said,
'OK, who moved my dog!'
Kirsty Roberts

What did the mummy bee say to her naughty baby?
Beehive yourself!
Stacey Hillman

What did the dog say when he sat on sandpaper?
Ruff!
Daniel Todd

What weighs a ton, loves smelly mud and laughs
a lot?
A happypotamus!
Laurence McGivern

Thank you to everyone who contributed
a joke, and to the following schools:

Abbey Hill Special School, Stoke-on-Trent
Adams School, Wem
Alderman Callow School, Coventry
Allesley Primary School, Coventry
Alverton School, Penzance
Balliol Lower School, Kempston
Bishop David Brown School, Woking
Bridlington Girls', Choir, Bridlington
Brotherton and Byram School, Knottingley
Cardross Primary School, Cardross
Cherry Willingham Community School, Lincoln
Christchurch Primary School, Bristol
Colton Hills Community School, Wolverhampton
Court Park Primary School, Hull
Dalziel High School, Motherwell
Faughan Valley High School, Londonderry
Gable Hall School, Stanford le Hope
Grangefield School, Stockton-on-Tees
Hazelbury Bryan Pre-school, Sturminster Newton
Humphry Davy School, Penzance
Kineton High School, Kineton
King's School, Worcester
Mile End School, Aberdeen
Morton School, Carlisle
New City Primary School, London

Priory School, Banstead
Quinton House School, Northampton
Richmond Park School, Glasgow
Roman Hill Middle School, Lowestoft
Shanklin Primary School, Isle of Wight
Shottermill Junior School, Haslemere
South Wirral High School, Wirral
Spellbrook Primary School, Bishop's Stortford
St Bartholomew's School, Quorn
St Bonaventure's Secondary School, London
St Cuthbert's High School, Johnstone
St Mary's High School, Waltham Cross
St Mary's Primary School, Failsworth
Stopsley High School, Luton
Tendring Technical College, Frinton-on-Sea
The Alice Ottley School, Worcester
The Sweyne Junior School, Swanscombe
Thornfield House School, Newtonabbey
Victory Christian Academy, Rugeley
Wellington School, Wellington
Westhoughton High School, Bolton
Ysgol Gogarth, Llandudno
Ysgol Morgn Llnyd, Wrexham

With apologies to anyone and any
organisation whose name appears
incorrectly spelled!

Child Of Achievement™ Awards
Annually presenting 150 Awards
and **giving** 150 grants to help **children** achieve **more**

150 Awards...

The Child Of Achievement™ Awards are now in their 20th year and are regarded as the most prestigious children's awards in the country. The Charity fund-raises to support the annual Awards and also makes grants and donations to help children achieve more in all walks of life.

The Awards are presented annually to 150 children up to the age of 16, who by their everyday tasks to help others or who by their ability to overcome illness or disability are worthy of the title "Child Of Achievement". The Child Of Achievement™ Awards recognises exceptional children, children who cope with a daily life that many adults would turn away from.

Our Award winners may be children who devote much of their young lives to caring for others or those who excel themselves at fundraising, putting the happiness of others before their own. Our winners are also those who endure painful and invasive medical treatments whilst still having a smile for those around them and going on to achieve more than was ever expected of them. Above all, our winners are an inspiration to others, a shining example of what can be achieved against seemingly insurmountable odds.

The children are selected from a huge yearly entry field of approximately 10,000 entries. All the 150 winners are equal winners. At the Awards' Ceremony, each child receives a certificate and a specially commissioned trophy and enjoys a party lunch at a leading London hotel. They also receive a photograph and an individual video to capture all the memories of the day. A number of well-known personalities and people in the public eye present the Awards to the children each year.

The Child Of Achievement™ Awards have been chosen as Airtours Charity of the year, with all fund-raising activities, including on-board collections focussed on helping children achieve more.

150 Grants...

150 Grants are presented every year to help children achieve more in all walks of life. Grants are available to families and organisations unable to meet all, or part of the cost of the grant request due to financial restraints.

Grants are given for a variety of requests, from equipment for children who are physically challenged to grants for children to enhance their skills in music and sport. Already we have contributed to medical equipment, given children who can't speak mechanical voices, provided electronic wheelchairs that really wheel and computers that are light activated. We have also funded special needs teachers enabling a whole class to achieve more.

We've also helped with money for school activities and practical help with funding where a child may take on the role of carer to a physically challenged adult, and needs someone to take their place while they take on school leisure activities.

We listen to every request and try really hard to help wherever we can.

To make a donation, nominate a child for an Award or apply for a grant, write to Child Of Achievement Awards, PO Box 86, Weybridge, Surrey, KT13 9JX
or Visit our Website: www.childofachievement.co.uk